Alfie
All Alone

Also by Holly Webb
Lost in the Snow
Lost in the Storm
Sam the Stolen Puppy

Alfie
All Alone

Holly Webb

Illustrated by Sophy Williams

SCHOLASTIC INC.

New York Toronto London Auckland Sydney
Mexico City New Delhi Hong Kong Buenos Aires

For Alice, Max, and Georgie

ISBN-13: 978-0-545-07925-9
ISBN-10: 0-545-07925-X

Text copyright © 2007 by Holly Webb
Illustrations copyright © 2007 by Sophy Williams

All rights reserved. Published by Scholastic Inc.,
557 Broadway, New York, NY 10012.
SCHOLASTIC and associated logos are trademarks and/or registered trademarks of Scholastic Inc. Lexile is a registered trademark of MetaMetrics, Inc.

12 11 10 9 8 7 6 5 4 3 2   9 10 11 12 13 14/0

Printed in the U.S.A.
First Scholastic printing, April 2009

Chapter One

"Evie, did you put these in the cart?" Evie's mom was staring at a package of rice cakes, looking confused.

"No. Why would I, Mom? They look horrible." Evie made a face. "It was you, don't you remember? You said they might be good to nibble on when you were feeling sick. But I bet they'll just make you feel even more sick."

Her mom sighed. "You're probably right." She smiled apologetically at the cashier who was waiting for them to pay. "Sorry. I seem to be a little forgetful at the moment."

The girl smiled back. "That's okay. My sister's pregnant, and she locked herself out of the house twice last week. How long until the baby's due?"

"Another nine weeks." Evie's mom sighed. "The time just seems to be creeping along at the moment." She patted her enormous tummy.

"Mom, can I go and look at the bulletin board?" Evie asked. She was getting bored hearing people talk about the baby. Ever since her mom's bump had begun to show, complete strangers had started talking to them in the street, asking about the baby. They always asked Evie how she felt about having a little brother or sister, and she was sick of having to smile and say she was looking forward to it. She was, but the fussing was starting to get on her nerves. And she had a horrible feeling that it would get a lot worse after the baby arrived.

"Of course you can. Actually, Evie, see if anyone's selling any baby stuff. It would be a good way to find some bargains."

Evie sighed quietly. Honestly, did Mom ever think about anything else? She wandered over to the big board behind the customer service desk, where people put up advertisements. You could find really fun things sometimes. Once she'd spotted an ad for a pair of nearly new Rollerblades that someone had outgrown. She'd been able to afford them with her pocket money, and they were great.

She browsed through vacuum cleaners, lawn mowers, a girl offering to babysit—and then caught her breath in delight. The next ad was larger than some of the others, and it had a photo attached: a basket of the cutest little white dogs, all clambering over each other. One of them was grinning out at Evie, a mischievous glint in his eye.

WESTIE PUPPIES READY FOR HOMES NOW REASONABLE PRICE

Call Mrs. Wilson at 555-5611

Evie sighed adoringly. That puppy was gorgeous! She had to show him to Mom. She looked back over at the checkout counter to see if she was done yet. Her mom was looking around for her. Evie waved and then dashed over.

"Come and see! You'll love it. Anyway, you shouldn't be pushing that on your own, Mom. Dad would be really angry." Evie helped her mom with the cart, giving her a stern glare.

"Dad is fussy." Mom chuckled. "What am I looking at?" She stared at the board, trying to figure out what Evie was so excited about. "We're not buying a trampoline, Evie," she said, grinning. "And we definitely don't want a speedboat!"

"No, look, I just wanted you to see this cute photo." Evie pointed out the basket of puppies. "Aren't they sweet?"

"Oh, yes, they're darling. What breed are they? Westies." Mom gazed thoughtfully at the photo. "Westies are fairly small dogs, aren't they?" she mused quietly.

Evie nodded. "I think Mrs. Jackson down the road has a Westie. You know, Tyson? He's great."

"Mmmm." Evie's mom nodded. "Okay. I suppose you're going to insist on pushing this cart now, aren't you? Actually, Evie, do you want to go and look at the animal magazines? I have to go to the ladies' room again." She sighed theatrically. "Don't move from the magazines, I'll only be a minute."

As soon as Evie set off, her mom quickly searched in her handbag for a pen. Then she wrote down the name and phone number from the puppy ad on her grocery receipt, and hurried after Evie.

As they drove home, Evie gazed out the window, daydreaming about puppies. She had no idea that her mom was sneaking glances at her every so often. Over the past few weeks, Evie's mom and dad had been worrying about how the new baby was going to affect her. After all, eight was quite old to suddenly have a new baby brother or sister. Evie seemed to be happy about it, but it was difficult to tell. They'd been wondering what they could do to keep her from feeling left out, and it was only the day before that Evie's dad had thought of getting her a puppy. Her mom hadn't been too sure.

"Won't it be a hassle, just before the baby comes?" she'd worried.

"We've got a few weeks. And the point is that Evie would be doing all the work—it'll give her something to fuss over when we're fussing over the baby."

Evie's dad was really enthusiastic. He liked dogs, and he knew Evie would love a puppy. After all, a puppy had been at the top of her Christmas list for the past three years. Her parents had always said she wasn't quite old enough, mostly because Evie's mom thought having a dog would be a lot of work. But Evie's dad had been trying hard to convince her, so the Westie ad had turned up at the perfect time.

"What are you thinking about, Evie?" Mom asked her, smiling. "You're miles away."

Evie grinned. "Just that adorable dog. I know we can't have a puppy, but if we could, I'd like one just like him."

Evie's dad got home just in time to help make dinner, and Evie told him about the little white dog as she was setting the table.

"Puppies? For sale now?" he asked thoughtfully.

Evie saw him exchange a glance with her mom and caught her breath, her eyes widening in sudden hope. She looked back and forth between them. Her dad was grinning. "Funny you should spot that ad today, Evie. Your mom and I were talking last night. We've been thinking about getting you a dog, and now seems like the right time."

Evie could hardly believe her ears.

"You mean it?" she asked them delightedly.

Mom nodded. "If you think you can

look after a dog properly. It's a big responsibility."

Evie nodded so hard she made her neck ache. "I know, I know. I can!"

Mom smiled. "So, should I call the lady with these puppies? You'd like a Westie?"

Evie just gaped at them. She'd wanted a dog for so long, and her parents had always said, "Maybe," and "Perhaps when you're older." Then she suddenly realized what her mom had just said and squeaked, "Yes! Yes, please!"

Evie hardly ate any dinner. She watched her parents eating impatiently, and when her dad had swallowed his last mouthful of pasta, she snatched the plate away to put in the dishwasher.

"Hey! Evie! I was going to have seconds!" He smiled. "Okay, okay. Let's put you out of your misery."

Evie waited anxiously while her mom called the number. What if all the puppies were gone? After all, they didn't know how long the advertisement had been up there. She sat on the stairs listening to her mom. It was difficult to figure out what was going on, but eventually her mom said, "Great. Well, we'll come around tomorrow morning. Thanks!" And then she put the phone down and beamed at Evie.

"I'm getting a puppy!" Evie gasped, jumping up and down in excitement. "I can't believe it! I have to go tell Gran!"

Evie's grandmother lived a couple of streets away, with her own two dogs, Ben the spaniel and Tigger, who was a greyhound mix. Evie heard them barking madly as she rang the doorbell. She grinned to herself. She couldn't wait to introduce Ben and Tigger to her new puppy!

"Guess what, guess what!" she yelled as Gran opened the door. "I'm getting a dog!" She didn't manage to say much after that since Tigger was jumping up and trying to lick her face.

"Down, Tigger! Stop it, silly boy. It's only Evie. You see her every day!" Gran shooed the dogs away and went into the kitchen to heat the tea kettle. "Darling, did you say you were getting a dog?"

"A puppy! Mom and Dad are giving me a puppy—we're going to pick one out tomorrow morning." Evie sighed blissfully. She wasn't sure she could wait that long.

Gran looked confused. "But . . . just before the baby arrives?"

Evie nodded happily. Then she leaned over the table, lowering her voice as though she were telling secrets. "They didn't say so, but I think it's to make me feel better about the baby," she explained.

Gran nodded thoughtfully. "Well, everyone would understand if you found it difficult, Evie. You know that, don't you?"

"Gran, you know I'm really looking forward to it." Evie laughed. "And now

I'll have a puppy as well!" She beamed at Gran, expecting her to be really excited. But Gran was stirring her tea thoughtfully. "What's the matter?" Evie asked, frowning.

"Nothing, Evie. It's good news. It's just—"Gran sipped her tea, thinking about what to say. "I'm just wondering if this is the right time. With the baby coming—a new puppy will be a lot of work, you know."

Evie shook her head. "Don't worry. I know about looking after dogs from helping with Ben and Tigger, and Dad knows lots about them, too." Evie bent down to scratch Tigger behind his ears, so she didn't see her grandmother's worried face. "I've wanted a dog for so long! I still can't believe it's really happening!" Evie gave Tigger an excited hug. Tomorrow she was going to meet her own puppy for the first time!

Chapter Two

Evie just couldn't stay in bed the next morning. She usually loved sleeping in on Saturdays after getting up for school all week, but today she was much too excited. She hardly ate any breakfast, either. She just stirred her chocolate cereal in circles till it looked like mud.

"You might as well eat it, you know,

Evie," her mom pointed out, slowly buttering a piece of toast. "We're not going yet. I told Mrs. Wilson we'd be there at ten."

"But that's hours away!" Evie wailed.

"Mrs. Wilson has to feed the puppies and clean their cage and get everything ready," her mom explained. "We can't go before then."

"I suppose not," Evie agreed. She trailed upstairs, wondering what she was going to do to fill a whole hour before they could leave. Then she had a great idea. She'd go and look up puppies on the Internet, and try to find out about looking after a dog. Evie settled down, and before long she was busy making notes. By the time her mom called her, Evie's head was bursting with information about feeding, walking, vaccinations, and training. It was a lot to think about. But she knew she could do it!

"Oh, look! He's so shy!" Evie giggled and stretched out her hand to the fluffy white puppy who was peeping out at her from behind his mother. He took a step back, then curiosity got the better of him. Tail slowly wagging, he began to sneak forward to where Evie was sitting on the floor.

"He's a little cutie, that one. Probably my favorite," Mrs. Wilson said fondly. "I'm going to miss him—he's such a sweet-natured dog."

Mom shook her head. "I don't know
how you can bear to see them go.
They're all so darling." She scratched
the puppy she was cuddling under the
chin, and the little dog sniffed happily
at her fingers.

"Well, this is the last time I'll have to, actually." Mrs. Wilson sighed. "Lady and I are getting too old for puppies! We're retiring, aren't we, my special girl?" She patted the puppies' mother, a beautiful snow-white dog with brown eyes that made her melt. "We're going to live by the sea. Lady loves walking along the beach. And getting soaking wet!"

Evie could have sworn that Lady's eyes sparkled naughtily. That was the amazing thing about her and the puppies—they all seemed so bright and intelligent. Then the fluffy little boy puppy suddenly nuzzled her hand, and she squeaked in delight. She'd been watching Lady and hadn't noticed him creeping up on her.

"He seems to have taken a shine to

you, Evie." Dad laughed, watching the puppy chasing Evie's fingers as she danced her hand up and down.

Evie nodded and then looked seriously at both Mom and Dad. "Is it really up to me to choose?" she asked worriedly. "I mean, all four of them are wonderful."

"It's a hard job," Dad agreed. "But we can't take them all."

Evie giggled as the little boy puppy mountaineered up her jeans, trying to climb into her lap. She helped him out with a boost under his little back paws, and he heaved himself up. Then he turned around four times, gave a big sigh of satisfaction, and went to sleep curled up tight in a little white ball.

Evie looked up, her eyes glowing. "This one," she said firmly.

"Mmm, I don't think you had much choice," Dad agreed, smiling. "He's definitely chosen you! Now you just have to think of a name for him."

Evie smiled. "I know what I'm going to call him. His name is Alfie."

Mom and Dad gazed at the little puppy. "That's a great name," said Mom. "He looks just like an Alfie."

It was hard to leave Alfie behind, but Evie knew she'd see him again the next day. He'd be coming home with them! Now they just had to get everything they needed to look after him. Mrs. Wilson had given them a list, and Evie studied it in the car on the way to the pet shop.

"Basket. Food bowl. Water bowl. Collar. Leash. Harness. Chew toys," she muttered.

Dad sighed. "Nearly as bad as the baby," he moaned. "Are you sure little Alfie doesn't need a crib as well, Evie?"

It was so exciting later that afternoon to see the basket with its pretty red cushion waiting in a warm spot in the kitchen, and the collar and leash hanging from one of the coat hooks in the hallway. Everything was ready for Alfie to come home.

"Oh, look, he's found his new basket!"

Evie and her parents were watching Alfie explore his new home. He was trotting around on unsteady paws, sniffing at everything.

"Achoo!" Alfie sneezed and stepped back, shaking his head.

"Ooops!" said Dad. "I didn't know my boots smelled that bad. Let's leave him to settle in."

That night, Evie sneaked back down to the kitchen after her bedtime to check if Alfie was okay. He'd eaten all his dinner and seemed to have made himself at home, but she was worried that he would be lonely. He was used to sleeping with his mom and his brother and sisters. Alfie had been lying awake, trying to make sense of all the strange things that had happened that day: his first car trip, a new house, a new basket to sleep in. And new people. They seemed very nice. The girl smelled friendly, which was very important.

The door clicked softly open and Alfie's ears pricked up. It was the girl, Evie. "Sssh!" she murmured. "We can't let Mom and Dad hear us, Alfie. You're supposed to stay in your basket, but I bet you're scared down here on your own. I'm taking you up to my bedroom instead. Mrs. Wilson said you were very well housebroken, so I'll put some newspaper down for you, okay? Mom would be mad if you wet my carpet!"

She snuggled him close as they crept up the stairs, and Alfie settled into her arms. This was much better than a basket, even the nice one he'd been given.

Of course, Evie's mom and dad soon figured out exactly what was going on, but they were so glad that Alfie was settling in and making Evie happy that they pretended not to notice. From then on, Alfie slept on Evie's bed every night, snoring gently.

It didn't take long for Alfie to become part of the family. He was such a friendly little dog! After a couple of weeks, when he'd had all his injections, he was allowed to go out for walks, which meant he could go to school to pick up Evie. She loved coming out to see Mom waiting with Alfie on his bright red leash. Usually it was twisted all around his paws, and he tripped over it as he tried to race over to her. Her friends were all really jealous, and Alfie got petted and stroked by everyone.

Then they'd head home and Alfie would watch TV with Evie on the sofa. He soon decided on his favorite programs, and he got very good at singing along to the theme songs in a tuneful howl.

Mom hadn't been so sure about getting a dog, but Alfie won her over very quickly. He loved people, and he followed her around as she did the housework. He was much better company than the radio! And whenever she sat down, he rested his head on her feet.

Of course, Alfie didn't have to work hard to charm Evie's grandmother. She was always popping over to see him and Evie, and it was great to have her to ask about dog-training tips. It only took Alfie a few days to learn about asking to go outside, and Gran warned Evie not to give him too many dog treats as a reward, since he was starting to look a bit chubby!

Once Alfie could be with other dogs, Evie took him to Gran's house to be introduced to Ben and Tigger. Alfie was a little shy at first—they were a lot bigger than he was, especially Tigger—but after half an hour he was chasing them around the yard. Ben the spaniel soon figured out a good way to calm Alfie down when he was being too puppyish and excitable—he sat on him! Evie panicked the first time he did it, but Gran said it would probably be good for Alfie to have an older dog bossing him around, and that Ben wouldn't hurt him.

Evie and Dad soon got into the habit of taking Alfie for an evening walk after dinner. It gave Mom a chance to snooze on the sofa in front of the television. Now that the baby was getting really big, she was tired a lot of the time. Dad and Evie always took a ball with them, or Alfie's favorite, a Frisbee. Dad had spotted it in the pet store and bought it for when Alfie was bigger, but once Alfie saw it, he didn't want to wait. So what if the Frisbee was almost as big as he was? He was very good at catching it. He took big leaps into midair, twisting and turning and snatching the Frisbee as it fell.

Then he'd haul it over the grass back to Evie and sit panting exhaustedly for a minute before yapping for them to throw it again. A couple of times he'd worn himself out so much that Dad had to carry him home and lay the exhausted puppy in his basket.

Evie was so happy that Alfie had become part of the family. She couldn't imagine life at home without him now.

Chapter Three

One night, Alfie was curled up snugly in a nest of blankets on top of Evie's toes. He was twitching happily in his sleep, dreaming of breakfast, when he was woken by the sound of Evie's parents talking. He sat up and listened carefully—it wasn't what he expected to hear in the middle of the night. Something interesting was going on. He padded up to the top of the bed and licked Evie's ear.

"Grrmmpf!" Evie wriggled and wiped the lick off her face. "Alfie! It's the middle of the night, silly. What are you doing?" She yawned and gave a little stretch. "Go back to sleep. It's hours till we have to get up." Then she turned over and snuggled her face back into her pillow.

Alfie huffed through his nose irritably. Why wouldn't Evie listen? Couldn't she tell that something exciting was happening? He took hold of Evie's pajama sleeve with his teeth very, very gently and pulled.

"Okay, Alfie, what is it?" she asked sleepily. "Do you need to go out? Because if you think I'm taking you all around the yard to find a good place at this time of night, you can think again!"

Alfie yapped sharply and tugged at Evie's sleeve again. Then he dropped the sleeve and stood silently, his ears pricked up.

Evie listened, and at last she understood why Alfie was behaving so strangely. Her parents weren't just talking now, they were moving around, too. Doors were opening and shutting quietly, and she could hear her dad on the phone to someone, sounding anxious. The baby was coming! It had to be that. Evie pulled her pillow up and leaned back against it, whispering to Alfie to come and sit with her. He burrowed in under her arm, and they listened together in the dark. Someone was arriving downstairs.

"That'll be Gran, I bet," Evie murmured. "They said they'd ask her to come and stay with me when they had to go to the hospital."

Alfie grunted in agreement. He liked

Gran. She had dog treats in her handbag.

A few minutes later, the front door banged open, and they heard someone coming up the stairs. At last Evie's bedroom door eased open, and Gran popped her head around.

"Hi, Gran!" Evie whispered.

"Hello, darling! I thought you might have woken up, with all the coming and going. I just came to check on you."

"Alfie woke me up. Is Mom having the baby now?" Evie sounded anxious.

Gran perched herself on the end of Evie's bed and stroked Alfie's nose.

"Clever Alfie. Yes, they think so. Don't get too excited, though—these things can take a while." She smiled down at Evie, still cuddling the little dog, and decided that she'd been wrong to worry. Evie loved him so much, and a dog would be just what her granddaughter needed to keep her company over the next few weeks.

The next day, Evie's parents brought baby Sam home. Evie's mom and Sam were both doing really well, and they didn't need to stay in the hospital. Mom said the noise of all the other babies in the nursery was driving her crazy, and she wanted to be home in her own bed.

Even though they were coming home as soon as they possibly could, the wait still seemed to last forever to Evie. It was a Saturday, so she was at home, with Alfie and Gran. The day really dragged, even though as a treat they all went to get fast food for lunch. Gran stood outside with Alfie, who was blissfully breathing in the smell of french fries, and Evie went in to get their food. When they got back, both Evie and Gran fed Alfie a few fries under the table, so he was soon full and fast asleep.

Evie couldn't help listening for the car—Dad had called to say they'd be home sometime that afternoon. They just had to wait for a doctor to give Mom one last check. Their street was pretty quiet, but Evie ran to the window to look at least ten times before she finally spotted their car pulling up.

"They're here!" she squeaked. Gran came hurrying over to join Evie. Evie's dad was trying to get the new baby seat out of the car, and all they could see of her new brother was a little bit of blue blanket trailing out of the seat.

Alfie couldn't tell what Evie was thinking, which was odd, because usually he had a good idea. Was she happy about this strange new thing that was happening? He licked her hand and made a questioning little "woof?" noise.

"That's the baby, Alfie. My brother, Sam. Let's go and see." Evie scrambled down from the windowsill, and Alfie trotted after her out into the hallway. Gran had opened the door, and Evie's parents were just bringing the baby in.

"Evie!" Mom hugged her tightly. "I missed you. Were you and Gran okay?"

"Of course. Can I see him, Mom?" Evie crouched down next to the baby seat and peered in. Sam seemed tiny inside—just a small hand clenched tightly around the blanket and a pale little face half-covered by a hat.

"Let's get him in and unwrap him, then you can really see him. It's a little chilly outside so he had to be covered up," Mom explained.

Alfie followed as the family went into the kitchen. The baby smelled new and different, and he wanted to investigate.

Gran and Evie watched as Mom undid Sam's little jacket, with Dad's help. At last she stood up and carried him over. "Do you want to sit down, Evie?" she asked. "Then you can cuddle him."

Evie whisked over to a chair and sat down, eagerly holding out her arms.

Mom kissed Sam's nose and handed him very carefully to Evie. "Sam, this is your big sister!"

Evie sat holding Sam, a look of amazement on her face. "He's smaller than some of my old dolls," she whispered, looking worriedly up at Mom. "Is he all right?"

Dad laughed. "He'll grow. You were littler than that."

Evie gazed down at Sam, watching as his eyes gradually opened. "He's looking right at me!" she squealed, beaming in delight.

Mom laughed. "I think he is! They say new babies can't really see much, but he's definitely staring at you."

"You know, he looks a lot like Evie," Dad said.

"Yes, I see what you mean," Gran agreed.

Alfie watched as they all chattered excitedly. He was feeling confused. No one had introduced him to the new baby. Evie was his person, and she was ignoring him. He gave a sharp little yap, and everyone jumped. The tiny creature on Evie's lap gasped and let out a shuddering wail that made Alfie back away. What was it?

"Alfie!" Evie said crossly. "What did you have to do that for? Look, you made Sam cry."

Alfie backed away still farther, his tail tucked between his legs. Now Evie was mad at him. He wasn't sure he liked this *baby* thing at all.

Over the next few days, Evie fell in love with her new little brother. Sam didn't do much except lie in a cradle and wail occasionally, but he was very cute. Evie's dad had some time off work to help out, so Evie had tried arguing that she ought to have time off school, too, but apparently it didn't work that way. She had to go back to school on Monday morning. Dad dropped her off in the car.

"You will bring Sam to pick me up, won't you?" she begged her mom. "I want everyone to see him. He's so much cuter than anyone else's little brothers and sisters."

The trip to pick up Evie from school was the first time Mom had taken Sam out in his new baby stroller. Alfie watched as Dad wrestled with the stroller. It would be nice to go for a walk. He'd been let out in the yard over the weekend, but no one had taken him for a real run, and he was eager to be out smelling some good smells. Alfie went to get his leash—it hung over a hook in the hall, and he could tug it down. He trotted back with it in his mouth just as Mom was maneuvering the stroller over the front step.

"You're sure you don't want me to come?" Dad asked again.

"No, you start making dinner. We'll be fine." And she closed the door behind her. Without Alfie!

Alfie barked to remind Mom that she'd left him behind. It wasn't like her to forget, but perhaps that baby had distracted her.

"Not today, Alfie." Dad shook his head. "Sorry, boy, but it's a bit much to have you *and* the stroller." He patted Alfie's head and went back into the kitchen, leaving Alfie in the hall, his leash still trailing out of his mouth.

Alfie stared at the door, confused. He always went to pick Evie up from school. Was Evie's mom really not coming back for him?

"Alfie! Biscuit!"

Evie's dad was calling. Alfie gave the door one last hopeful look. Oh, well. He supposed a biscuit was better than nothing.

When Mom and Evie got back from school they were both looking a bit frazzled. Sam had snoozed most of the way and then woken up just in time for everyone to say how cute he was, but now he was hungry and unhappy, and a thin wailing noise was coming from his nest of blankets.

Mom sat on the sofa to feed him, and Evie curled up next to her to watch— she'd really missed seeing Sam while she was at school. Alfie jumped up, too. He thought they were going to watch television together, like they usually did. But Evie squeaked in horror and pushed him off. "Alfie, no! You might squash Sam!"

Alfie's tail drooped, and he slunk miserably into the kitchen. The baby was going to watch all his favorite programs with Evie instead. It wasn't fair.

All the next week, people kept coming by with presents for the new baby, and sometimes one for Evie, too. Everyone seemed to think Sam was very special, and he got fussed over all the time. Alfie wasn't quite sure why. Sam didn't do a lot, and he certainly couldn't do tricks like a dog could. Alfie couldn't help wishing that things would go back to normal and everyone would fuss over him instead, but he had a feeling it wasn't going to happen.

But at least Alfie had been able to reclaim his place on the sofa. Mom said she thought it was okay for

Alfie to sit there when she was feeding Sam, if Evie was careful not to let Alfie lick him.

"Alfie's used to sitting there with you, Evie," she pointed out. "It isn't fair if he's not allowed to anymore. Just keep an eye on him." She sat Sam up to get him to burp, and she smiled. "Look, Sam's watching Alfie's tail wag. I think he'll love having Alfie for company."

Evie scratched Alfie behind the ears, and he settled down on her lap, keeping a watchful eye on the baby. He supposed he didn't mind sharing the sofa.

Chapter Four

"Evie! Evie! You're going to be late for school!" Mom was calling up the stairs, sounding unhappy. She had Sam tucked under one arm, and he was unhappy, too. "You won't have time for breakfast!"

Evie stomped down the stairs looking very gloomy. "I don't want any. And I don't want to go to school, either. I don't feel very well. I'm really tired."

Evie's mom took a deep breath and counted to five. "I know. We all are. But it's Friday. You can sleep in over the weekend."

"If Sam doesn't keep me awake all night, like he did last night," Evie growled.

"It's not his fault, Evie. He doesn't understand the difference between night and day yet." Mom was sounding really strained.

"Well, can't you teach him?" Evie looked up at her mom and suddenly grinned. "Oh, all right. I suppose not. But I am really, really tired." She sighed and hooked her finger into Sam's tiny hand. "Don't you dare nap all afternoon, Sam. Stay up, and then you'll sleep tonight!"

It hadn't been a good week. Evie's dad was back at work now, and it was harder to get everything done without the extra help. Sam was beautiful, but he wasn't sleeping well, and when he was awake he was loud. Everyone's temper was fraying.

Alfie was trying his best to keep out of the way, but he never managed to be in the right place. Most days Evie's mom walked into him about three times just doing the dishes. When she got back from taking Evie to school that Friday, she tripped over Alfie while she was carrying a basket of laundry, and stepped on his paw, but she didn't seem to be sorry. He held it up and whined, but all she did was snap, "Alfie! Not again! Get out of the way, you silly dog!"

Alfie limped out of the kitchen, feeling sorry for himself.

He sat in the hallway, thoughtfully chewing on a small teddy bear he'd found on the stairs. He just couldn't seem to do anything right anymore. Things had been much nicer before.

At that moment, Sam started crying upstairs. Mom dashed past to go get him and saw the small pile of shredded fur that had once been a teddy. "Alfie!" she wailed, and Alfie gazed up at her. He didn't know why she was angry—furry toys were there to be chewed, and he didn't see what the fuss was about. But it looked like Mom didn't agree, judging by the way she snatched up what was left of the teddy and glared at him.

Alfie was still in the doghouse when Gran came by that afternoon, and he was delighted to see her. At last, someone actually had time to sit and scratch him behind the ears! He leaned against Gran's leg sweetly. For a moment he almost wished that she would take him back to her house. Then he shook his head and snorted. No! He was Evie's dog. He was sure that she would get over the baby thing soon, and then maybe they could go back to real walks and more cuddling.

"You look exhausted!" Gran was saying to Mom. "Why don't you go upstairs and have a nap? I'll look after Sam for you."

Mom sighed. "I'd love to, but he's being so grumpy today. He wouldn't even go to his dad this morning. Every time I put him in his crib he howls. I just don't know what's the matter with him. Anyway, I've got to go get Evie in a minute."

Gran stood up firmly. "Put him in the stroller, and I'll take him with me and get Evie for you. You go and have a rest. Sam will probably sleep, too."

"If you're sure . . ." Mom tucked Sam in and went upstairs, looking grateful.

Me, too! Me, too! Alfie whined hopefully, bouncing around Gran's ankles as she headed for the door. He was desperate for more walks.

"Sorry, Alfie, I'd love to take you, but I'm not used to this stroller and I can't manage both of you." She looked down at the little dog thoughtfully. "I'd better talk to Evie about you. I don't think she's exercising you enough."

Alfie yelped in agreement, and she nodded to herself.

Unfortunately, Gran's master plan for calming down Sam didn't work. At five o'clock, when she had to leave to go feed Tigger and Ben, Sam was still wailing. And when Evie's dad walked in at six, he was greeted by a howling baby, a frazzled wife, and a grumpy daughter.

"Looks like we're in for a fun weekend," he joked, but nobody else thought it was funny.

Alfie watched Dad hopefully. Mom and Evie had been so stressed by Sam's crying that they had forgotten to feed him. He nosed eagerly at his food bowl and looked up at Dad. He wasn't watching. Alfie sighed and trailed back to his basket, where he curled up with his back to the rest of the family. Maybe he'd better just take a nap and try again in a while.

A couple of hours later, Alfie was convinced he was going to starve if he didn't get fed soon. He trotted into the living room, where Mom and Dad were taking turns walking Sam up and down. Evie was just getting ready to go up to bed. Alfie was horrified. If Evie went to bed, they'd never remember to feed him! Desperate measures were needed. He nipped back to the kitchen.

"Oh, thank goodness," Mom murmured, watching as Sam slumped slightly on his dad's shoulder. "He's going to sleep. No, don't stop!"

Dad nodded grimly and resumed his trek up and down the room. "I think he's fallen asleep," he said, a couple of minutes later. "Can we risk laying him down, do you—"

It was at that moment that Alfie trotted back in, carrying his metal food bowl in his teeth. He dropped it hard on the wooden floor and barked.

Sam shot upright and let out a bloodcurdling wail.

"Alfie! You bad dog!" Mom groaned. "That's it. Kitchen! Now! In your basket!" And she shooed him out, flapping her hands crossly.

Alfie was banished. It was the first night he'd ever spent in the kitchen, instead of curled up on the end of Evie's bed. He was so confused. He'd only wanted his dinner! Everyone else had had theirs, and he was starving.

For the next hour, Alfie and Sam howled together. Then Sam suddenly decided not to bother anymore and fell blissfully asleep, but Alfie lay in his basket and stared at the dark kitchen. Why didn't Evie want him upstairs? What had he done?

Didn't she love him anymore?

Chapter Five

The next morning was Saturday, and the family was having breakfast. It was always a really nice time—the beginning of the weekend, when they all had a chance to relax. They usually had something extra nice for breakfast, too. Today, not even croissants could cheer everyone up.

At least Sam seemed to be in a better

mood. He was sitting in his bouncy chair in the living room.

"He's fine," Dad reported back after a quick check. "Seems to be enjoying himself, actually. I think he's learning to bat at that dangly toy you bought him, Evie." He gave a long, slow sigh of relief, sat down, and poured himself a large cup of coffee.

Alfie jumped up, his paws on Dad's knee, holding his squeaky bone hopefully in his mouth. Dad was usually good for a game.

"Not now, Alfie," Dad muttered, pushing him away gently.

Alfie went to paw at Evie's ankles, hoping for a bit of croissant. She dangled a piece by his nose, and he gulped it down gratefully.

"Evie!" Mom said sharply. "Are you giving Alfie scraps? How many times have I told you not to feed that dog at the table?" Mom didn't normally mind that much, but today she was tired and snappish.

"Shoo, Alfie!" Evie whispered, nudging him out from under the table with her foot.

Alfie took one look at Mom's face and trailed sadly into the living room. He sat down next to Sam. The baby was half smiling at the bouncy toy stretched across the front of his chair, and vaguely waving a hand at it every so often. Alfie watched. It was fun. He lay down with his nose on his paws and gazed up as the little creatures jumped and danced.

Sam smelled nice—milky—and he was relaxing to be with after the tense, grumpy mood in the kitchen. Sam made little squeaky, grunting noises to himself, and Alfie woofed quietly back, his eyes slowly closing as he drifted off for a snooze.

After a few minutes, the jingling of the toy was joined by an irritating buzz. Alfie opened one eye. Was it Sam making that noise? Was he supposed to do that? No, Sam was asleep. The buzzing was from a large fly that had landed on the baby's arm. Alfie bristled as he watched it crawl over Sam. He hated flies, and he knew Evie's mom did, too. Whenever a fly buzzed nearby she always shooed it away. That fly should *not* be crawling over Sam.

Alfie watched, waiting for his moment to pounce. He was so intent on the fly that he had no idea Evie and her mom had come into the living room to check on Sam. They watched in horror as Alfie pounced, his sharp white teeth snapping on the fly, just inches away from Sam's arm.

"Alfie, no!" Evie screamed as her mom threw herself forward to grab Sam away.

Alfie had never heard Evie sound like that before—terrified and angry at the same time. He shot under the sofa and lay there cowering.

Sam hadn't noticed the fly, but he certainly noticed when his mom snatched him out of his nice sleep. He roared angrily and waved his arms around.

"Mom, is he okay? I can't believe Alfie tried to bite him!" Tears were rolling down Evie's cheeks.

Evie's mom was breathing fast. From where she and Evie had been standing, it really had looked as though Alfie had meant to bite Sam's arm, and she'd been terrified. She was pushing up the sleeve of his pajamas, searching for marks, but he seemed fine—just upset at being woken.

"What happened? Are you all right?" Evie's dad rushed into the room, bathrobe flapping. "Is something the matter with Sam?" he asked, taking in the scene.

"No. No, we're all okay," Evie's mom said slowly.

"Dad, Alfie nearly bit Sam!" Evie sobbed, throwing her arms around him. She couldn't believe that her sweet puppy would do such a horrible thing—but then she'd seen it with her own eyes— she'd watched him jump at her baby brother, teeth bared.

"I don't think he did, Evie." Mom

sounded as though she was trying to figure it all out. "Look."

Lying on the floor next to the bouncy chair was a huge horsefly, legs in the air, still buzzing faintly.

"You know how Alfie hates flies. He's always snapping at them. I think he just tried to catch a fly that had landed on Sam's arm."

Evie lifted her head from where it was buried in her dad's robe. "Really?"

Evie's dad was looking serious. "Are you sure?"

"Well, no, I suppose not. But Alfie's never done anything like that before, has he?"

Evie shook her head, smiling in relief. "Never! Oh, Mom, thank goodness you saw that fly. We'd never have known otherwise."

"Where is Alfie?" Dad asked, looking around.

"I shouted at him, and he disappeared under the sofa!" Evie went pale. "Oh, he must think we're so angry! Poor Alfie." Evie crouched down to look, but Alfie flinched away from her and retreated all the way to the back. Evie sat up, looking hurt. "He won't come," she said miserably.

"You probably need to give him a little more time." Dad put an arm around her, and the other around Mom and Sam. "Come on into the kitchen."

Alfie huddled under the sofa, trembling. No one had ever shouted at him like that before. Evie had behaved as though he'd done something terrible. But he'd been helping Sam! Evie's mom was always saying that flies were horrible, dirty things. She waved them away if they got anywhere near the baby.

Did Evie and Mom think I was trying to bite Sam? Alfie wondered. *I'd never do that! Don't they know I'd never do that?* Alfie lay there, feeling confused. No one seemed to understand him very much here anymore. He was always in trouble, and even Evie, who used to love him so much, didn't seem to have any time for him. Maybe they really did think he was the sort of dog who would bite.

"Alfie! Alfie!" Evie was calling him. She was lying down, peering under the sofa. "Come out, Alfie, please? I didn't mean it. Please come out, I'm so sorry for shouting at you." Her eyes met his hopefully, and Alfie couldn't hold back any longer.

He crept forward, tail slowly starting to wag. As he wriggled out from under the sofa, she hugged him tight, burying her face in his thick white fur. "Oh, Alfie." Alfie put his paws on her shoulders and licked her face, tasting salt from her tears. Why was she crying? Everything was all right now. He wagged his tail and licked her again lovingly.

"Ugh, Alfie!" Evie giggled and sniffed. "I'm covered in saliva. Oh, I do love you." She sighed. "I'm so sorry. I haven't been showing it much, have I?"

Alfie woofed encouragingly. He adored Evie, and he trusted her. Hearing the love in Evie's voice as he snuggled against her was all he needed to feel better.

Chapter Six

The rest of the day was almost perfect for Alfie. Evie seemed to be back to her old self. She cuddled him a lot, and she kept saying she was sorry for thinking he'd hurt Sam. She told him what a smart dog he was for catching the fly. But every so often, Alfie would remember how upset and angry everyone had been and shudder, and then Evie would hug him all over again.

Only one thing spoiled it. Alfie kept catching worried looks between Evie's mom and dad—worried looks directed at him. Maybe they thought he was still frightened. He tried to be extra bouncy and friendly, with lots of jumping up to lick them, but it didn't seem to work. If anything, they looked more worried, although they always patted him and smiled.

Evie gave him a huge dinner, and Alfie was so full afterward that he went to sleep on her lap while she was trying to finish her homework at the kitchen table. He didn't notice when Evie's parents came to sit with her, or see the anxious looks on their faces.

"Evie." Mom sounded strangely

nervous. "Evie, we have to talk to you, sweetheart."

Evie looked up. "I'm doing it! Look, I'm doing it now. It's only Saturday, Mom. I'll get it done, easily!"

"Not about your homework." Dad's voice was really flat, and Evie looked at him, suddenly scared. This was far more serious than just them complaining that she was rushing through her homework at the last minute.

"It's about Alfie," Dad went on.

Her heart suddenly thumping, Evie put her hand down to pet Alfie, curled on her lap. He gave a little whine of pleasure and stretched out luxuriously in his sleep before curling himself up again even tighter.

"What's the matter?" Evie asked
quietly.

Her mom and dad exchanged a look, then her dad sighed. "We're not sure we can keep him, Evie."

Evie gulped, her hand tightening on Alfie's neck so that he wriggled uncomfortably. "Why?" she whispered. Then her voice strengthened. "He wasn't biting, Dad, really," she assured him. "He wouldn't do that." She smiled desperately at her dad, knowing she had to convince him.

"Evie, you thought he would," Dad said gently. "And so did your mom. You were so upset this morning."

"But he didn't! It was all a mistake." Evie's eyes were filling with tears. Her dad sounded so decided. She turned to her mom for help and saw that she was crying, too.

"It's not Alfie's fault at all. It's just that we haven't been able to take good care of Alfie, Evie," her mom said shakily. "We all love him, but he needs real walks and lots of attention. He hasn't been getting that. Dogs can get very grumpy if they're cooped up in the house all day."

"I'll walk him more!" Evie cried out. "Every day! Twice a day. I've just been paying so much attention to Sam, that's all."

"We all have," her dad agreed. "But that's not fair to Alfie. He needs a home where he doesn't get forgotten."

"I didn't mean to!" Evie wailed so loudly that Alfie woke up, his little white head suddenly popping up at the table, making them all giggle hopelessly. He gave them a happy, doggy smile, showing lots of long pink tongue. What was the joke? Then he looked again, turning to sniff at Evie. Maybe there wasn't a joke at all. Something felt wrong. Had he done something bad again? He hunched down onto Evie's lap, looking scared.

"Evie, look at him. He's upset. It's not fair to put him through that," Evie's mom said gently.

Evie sniffed. "If—if we're not going to keep him, what are we going to do? Are you going to give him back to Mrs. Wilson?" She gulped, imagining Alfie sitting sadly in the puppy room all on his own, his brother and sisters already gone to new homes.

"No." Dad looked thoughtful. "It would have been the best option, but she's stopped breeding dogs now. She's retired to the seaside, remember?"

"I suppose she might take Alfie back," Mom said. "Oh, but we don't have her new address."

"I think the sensible thing would be to take him to Riverside," Dad said firmly, as though trying to convince himself.

"Riverside?" Evie's eyes filled with tears again. "Where Gran got Ben and Tigger? But that's for dogs that people don't want! We *do* want Alfie!"

"Dogs that people can't keep, Evie." Mom's voice sounded so sorry that Evie knew there was no point arguing. Hugging Alfie to her, she jumped up and raced up the stairs to her room.

Evie didn't come down for dinner. Alfie had already had his huge dinner, and he was delighted to stay upstairs with Evie all evening. She was paying him lots of attention, teasing and tickling him, and playing all his favorite games. At bedtime he was allowed to snuggle up on her bed again. Alfie heaved a deep, happy sigh. This was where he was meant to be, not down in the kitchen on his own. Everything was the way it should be. He fell asleep at once, worn out from all the playing, so he didn't notice that Evie lay awake half the night, tears rolling silently down her cheeks.

"Evie, you don't have to come."

Alfie looked with interest back and forth between Evie and Dad. They were going somewhere! Excellent! He trotted off to fetch his leash, and jumped up with his paws on Evie's knees to give it to her.

Evie gulped, and tears started to seep from the corners of her eyes again. He was such a darling dog! How could they be doing this? Hurriedly she wiped the tears away—she didn't want Alfie to know what was going on. "I'm coming," she said firmly, her voice hardly shaking at all. "I'm not having Alfie think I didn't say good-bye."

Dad sighed. "Okay. Hey, Alfie, come on, boy. You're going on a car ride," he said, trying to sound cheerful.

But Alfie laid his ears back. Something odd was going on. He jumped into the car and saw that Evie's hands were trembling as she fastened his harness. Usually Evie would beg her dad to have the radio on and they'd sing along, but today they hardly spoke at all.

When the car stopped, Alfie thought Evie would put his leash on and let him walk, but for some reason she was carrying him up in front of her so she could nuzzle into his fur. Alfie licked her face gratefully. He liked being carried; he could see what was going on. Evie was walking very slowly, though. Dad kept stopping and looking back at her as they headed toward the building. Alfie wasn't surprised. It didn't smell good. It was too clean, like the vet's that he'd been taken to a few weeks before.

What was this place?

Evie stood by the reception desk while Dad explained quietly to a girl in a green uniform. She was nodding sympathetically, and she gave Alfie a considering look.

"I'm sure he'll find a new home very quickly. He's a pretty little dog." She came around the desk and held out her arms. "Come on, sweetie," she crooned to Alfie.

Alfie suddenly felt scared. Who was this girl? Why were they here? All at once he knew that the lovely, cuddly time he'd been having with Evie for the past day hadn't been real. In fact, nothing had been right since he'd snapped at that fly on Sam's arm. But he didn't understand! What should he have done? He twisted helplessly as the girl in green lifted him from Evie's arms. He was squealing with fright, desperately trying to get away.

"Come on, Evie." Her dad quickly marched Evie away before she could grab Alfie back again. Alfie's last sight of Evie was as her dad hustled her out the door, hugging her tightly against him so that she couldn't turn and see her little dog howling for her to come back.

Chapter Seven

As Evie trailed up the front path, she heard someone calling her, and excited woofs. She spun around immediately, thinking that somehow it was Alfie.

"Hello, Evie! Ben and Tigger and I are just out for our walk. We thought we'd see if you and Alfie wanted to come with us. I know you haven't had a lot of time to walk him recently."

Gran was beaming at Evie, but then she noticed Evie's dad, who was shaking his head and holding a finger to his lips.

"Jack, are you all right?" Gran asked worriedly as Tigger and Ben towed her through the gate.

Evie's dad sighed. "Not really."

Evie crouched down to pat Ben and Tigger. "We just took Alfie to Riverside," she told them quietly. Somehow it was easier to tell the dogs than Gran. Suddenly, she remembered. "You were right, Gran, you said we wouldn't be able to take care of Alfie."

"Oh, sweetheart, I'm really sorry." Gran's face crumpled. "I hadn't realized it was that bad. Why didn't you tell me?" she asked Evie's dad.

He shrugged. "It was one of those difficult decisions," he said sadly. "I'm sure someone really nice will take Alfie home. You know that, Evie, don't you?"

Evie was fighting back tears. She didn't want anybody else taking Alfie anywhere, even if they fed him out of a solid gold bowl! He was her dog—only he wasn't. Not anymore. In fact, she suddenly realized, she was never going to see him again. She gasped, and then she scrambled up and dashed into the house, tears stinging her eyes.

"That little Westie's still not eating."

"Really? He's only been here three days. He'll change his mind soon."

Two girls in green Riverside uniforms leaned against the wall, sipping their coffee and staring thoughtfully into Alfie's cage. He was curled up at the back, a miserable little ball, not even looking at his overflowing food bowl.

"He's really taking it hard, poor little thing."

"Yeah. I was here when they brought him in—the little girl he belonged to was really upset, too."

Alfie snuggled his paws farther around his ears to shut out their voices. If he kept his eyes shut tight, he could almost pretend that he was back home.

"Alfie! Alfie!"

Alfie twitched, but it wasn't Evie. It was another of the Riverside staff, with some people looking for a dog. Quite a few people had been to see Alfie already, and everyone said how cute he was. They seemed surprised, as though such a sweet puppy shouldn't really be at a dogs' home. But when they tried to talk to Alfie and he refused to budge from the back of his cage, they gave up, moving on to friendlier dogs.

"Mom, look at this great dog!" A boy about Evie's age was peering through the fence. "Can we meet him? Please?"

"Sure." The Riverside girl got out her keys. "This is Alfie. He's a gorgeous Westie puppy who is available because his owners had a new baby and couldn't keep him. He's a darling boy, but he's not too happy right now. Hey, Alfie." She cooed gently to him. "Come and meet Ethan, he's looking for a nice dog just like you."

Alfie hunched himself up tighter. The staff at Riverside were right. He hadn't accepted what was going on. How could he? He didn't understand. He couldn't let anyone take him home because Evie was coming back for him. He was sure of it. But he was becoming just a little less sure every time he woke up and he was still in a cage, waiting for her.

The girl picked him up, and Alfie lay limply and sadly in her arms as she carried him out. The little boy stroked him gently. "He's great."

Ethan's eyes were shining, just like Evie's used to. Alfie let Ethan scratch him behind the ears. That was nice.

"Can we take him home?" Ethan begged.

Home! Alfie suddenly twisted in the Riverside girl's arms and growled angrily. What was he thinking? His home was with Evie.

Ethan's parents pulled him away quickly to look at another dog, and the girl with the keys sighed. "Oh, Alfie. That would have been a wonderful home. When are you going to give up and let someone else love you?"

Alfie slunk back into his cage, and curled up facing the wall. He only wanted Evie to love him.

Evie thought it was strange that her house could feel so different just because Alfie wasn't there. She didn't have a warm body curled on her toes at night. No cold nose was resting on her knee at mealtimes, hoping for scraps. Only Mom and Sam met her from school, and she and Dad didn't go for walks anymore. Alfie's going away had changed everything.

She tried to explain to Gran when she went to her house after school on Wednesday.

"I never really thought about how nice it was having Alfie to play with when Mom was busy. She's got so much to do with feeding Sam and everything. But I had Alfie, and it was okay. I really miss him, Gran." She stared into her juice, and Tigger pushed his head into her lap, sensing that she was unhappy. "Yeah, you miss him, too, don't you, Tigger?"

"I think your parents must miss Alfie as well, you know," Gran said.

Evie nodded miserably. "I think Dad does. I caught him in the hall yesterday with Alfie's leash. He looked really confused, and he muttered something about having forgotten. We sometimes used to take Alfie for walks after dinner."

"Why don't you talk to them about it?

You might have made the wrong decision." Gran looked thoughtfully at Evie, wondering what she'd say.

Evie pet Tigger. Then she looked up, and her face was so sad that Gran caught her breath. "I should never have let him go, Gran!" She got up to put on her coat. "I miss Alfie so much."

Gran nodded firmly. "I definitely think you should talk to them." She watched Evie walking slowly down the path, and then she looked down at Ben and Tigger. They stared back at her encouragingly. "Mmm. Yes, I think you're right," Gran muttered to herself.

A couple of times during the week, Evie thought about what Gran had said, but there didn't seem any point in talking to Mom and Dad about Alfie. It would just make everything worse when they said no, and she was sure she wouldn't be able to change their minds. Then on Saturday morning she wandered into the kitchen and found her mom staring at something on the table, with a funny look on her face.

"What's the matter?" Evie leaned over to see what she was looking at. Her mom was holding a photo of Alfie.

"Oh! Evie, I didn't hear you come in." Mom quickly put the photo back on the windowsill, but Evie was staring at her.

"You miss him, too, don't you?" she asked, her voice suddenly full of hope. "Gran said you did, but I didn't believe her." Then her shoulders slumped. "But I suppose it doesn't make any difference." She looked over at Sam, who was sitting in his bouncy chair staring in wonder at his toes. She still adored her baby brother, but she couldn't help thinking that it was his fault.

Mom looked, too. "Maybe." Then her voice changed. "Maybe not, Evie. Perhaps we were being too hard on him."

"Who?" Dad walked in with the newspaper. "Got you some chocolate, Evie," he added, throwing her a bar.

Evie caught it automatically but didn't

even look to see what kind it was. "Dad, Mom thinks maybe we shouldn't have taken Alfie to Riverside!"

Her dad sat down at the table slowly, looking back and forth between them. "Really?" he said thoughtfully.

Mom sat down, too. "Come on. Tell me you haven't missed him."

"But that's not the point! We weren't able to take care of him. And what about Sam? Think back to this time last week!"

"I think we overreacted. We panicked. We were all tired, and we made a snap decision. I don't think it was a good one." Mom reached for his hand. "Alfie was such fun to have around. Do you really think he would have harmed Sam?"

Evie watched hopefully, holding her breath as Dad shook his head. "To be honest, I think watching Alfie cheered the little guy up sometimes," he said.

They looked over at Sam, who stared back seriously and said, "Ooooo," in a meaningful way, waving his foot.

"And I really missed taking him to the newsstand this morning," Dad added. "You know, I never came out of that store and found Alfie on his own. He was always being fussed over by someone. Everyone loved him."

Evie took a deep breath. "So can we go and get him back?" she asked, twisting her fingers together anxiously.

Dad looked serious. "It wasn't just about Sam though, Evie. We'd need to take better care of Alfie." He exchanged a glance with Mom. "We need to think this through."

Mom nodded. "Evie, could you do me a big favor and change Sam's diaper?"

"Now?" Eve sounded disbelieving.

"Yes, now." Mom smiled at her. "Your dad and I need to talk. And Sam needs a diaper change."

Evie picked Sam up, making a face, and carried him upstairs.

When Evie got back, Mom and Dad were looking at the photo of Alfie again. "Have you decided?" Evie asked hopefully, cuddling Sam close.

"Do you think we can all be better owners for Alfie this time around?" Dad asked.

"Yes! And Gran would help!" Evie reminded him. "She said she would. I could take him out for walks with her and Ben and Tigger."

"No getting grumpy with Alfie just because Sam's made us tired."

"No! I promise. Pleeease! Can we have him back?"

Dad grinned at her. "Okay. Let's go and get Alfie!"

Evie and her parents were talking excitedly in the car about how great it would be to have Alfie back when Dad suddenly stopped in the middle of his favorite story about Alfie trying to catch a pigeon.

"I just had a thought," he said quietly. "It's possible someone else has already given Alfie a new home. He's been at Riverside a week, and he's such a beautiful dog. Evie, I don't want to upset you, but it's possible Alfie's gone."

Evie gulped. "Can you drive faster?"

Evie and her dad jumped out of the car as soon as they got to the rescue center, while Mom wrestled with Sam and the stroller. "You go!" she said, waving them on.

They dashed into the reception area, and Dad explained why they had come back, while Evie hopped up and down impatiently. The girl at the desk was taking a long time to bring up Alfie's file on the computer. At last Evie couldn't stand it. She slipped through the big double door that led to the dogs' kennels. She had to tell Alfie he was coming home!

But Alfie wasn't there.

Chapter Eight

"And they wouldn't tell you who'd taken him?" Mom asked indignantly.

"Well, no. I can see why not. We gave Alfie up. It wouldn't be fair to his new owners if we could just storm in and take him home," Dad pointed out.

Mom sighed. "I suppose not. But it seems so unfair."

"Can we not talk about it?" came a small voice from the backseat. Evie was sadly dangling a toy in front of Sam's car seat, and he was giggling, the only member of the family feeling cheerful.

"Sorry, Evie. You're right, it's not going to change anything. At least we're going to Gran's. That'll make us feel better. I'll bet she's made a cake."

Evie stared at the car ceiling, concentrating on not snapping at her parents. They were only trying to be nice—but honestly, a cake? That was supposed to make it all right that she'd just lost her wonderful dog forever? Evie sniffed hard. She didn't want to start crying again. She'd just managed to stop, and her eyes were hurting. She loved Gran, but she wished they weren't going to her house today. Gran would never have let anything like this happen to Ben or Tigger, and seeing them was just going to make Evie miss Alfie more.

He's with a nice family, she told herself firmly. *He'll have a great time. The Riverside people wouldn't give him to anyone who wouldn't take care of him. Someone like us*, she couldn't help adding.

Evie had never noticed how many dogs lived in the few streets between her house and Gran's, but that afternoon they seemed to be everywhere. As they turned the corner onto Gran's street, she could hear excited yapping, and something tugged in her heart. It sounded just like Alfie. But it was only Ben and Tigger, playing in the front yard. Gran let them out there sometimes for a change.

Dad put his arm around Evie's shoulders. "You can still come and play with these two, you know," he said sympathetically.

Evie nodded. But it wasn't the same as having her own dog. She'd never noticed before how much Ben sounded like Alfie, though. It was weird that he had that same squeaky bark. Actually, he probably didn't—she was just going to imagine Alfie everywhere for a while. *I wonder how long that will last?* Evie thought to herself miserably. *Forever, I suppose.* She leaned over the gate to undo the latch, and the dogs bounded over to say hello.

All three of them.

"Alfie!" Evie gasped, finally realizing that the squeaky bark sounded like Alfie because it *was* Alfie. It was Alfie jumping twice his own height to try to get over the gate to greet her. "Alfie!" She fought with the latch, but she was crying so much that Dad had to open it for her. Alfie shot into her arms and tried to lick her all over, his woofs getting squeakier than ever with excitement.

You came back! You came back! he was saying, if Evie could have understood him.

"I don't understand," Evie said dazedly, as they sat around the table. Mom had been right, there was a delicious-looking cake, although at the moment only Alfie seemed interested in it. He was perched on Evie's knee, gradually easing himself closer and closer to one of the delicious chocolaty bites.

Gran smiled. "Well, after I talked to you, Evie, I changed my mind. I thought you were not ready to have a dog—it's such a huge responsibility. But then, with Alfie gone, you seemed so sad. And I love Alfie, too. I decided that even if you didn't feel you could have him back right now, with Sam so little, then I would keep him myself and you could visit him. Ben and Tigger like having a bouncy young pup to cheer them up." She looked over at her dogs, who were slumped exhaustedly on their cushions. Tigger seemed to have his paws over his eyes. "Mmmm. Well, the extra exercise is good for them."

"We can take him home, can't we? He can live with us, like Gran said. And Gran can help us out if we're having a problem?" Evie asked her parents anxiously.

"Definitely!" said her dad. "Alfie's part of the family. Aren't you, boy?" Then he laughed. "And Sam thinks so, too."

Sam was sitting on Mom's lap, next to Evie and Alfie. He was leaning over toward Alfie, his fingers clumsily batting at Alfie's shiny collar tag so that it jingled and flashed in the sun. Sam gurgled happily, enjoying his game. Alfie shook his ears and snorted gently, edging slightly closer on Evie's knee so Sam could reach.

Evie smiled down at him, hugging him tightly. Alfie knew that he was home for good.

Animal Rescue

Tina Nolan

Abandoned . . . lost . . . neglected?
There's always a home at Animal Magic!

In a perfect world there'd be no need for
Animal Magic. But Eva and Karl Harrison,
who live at the animal rescue center with their
parents, know that life isn't perfect. Every day
there's a new arrival in need of their help!

Charlie
The home-alone kitten

Everything's going well for Animal Magic's
Open House until the celebrity guest, soccer
star Jake Adams, cancels at the last minute.
Eva plays detective, but when she arrives at
Jake's house all she finds is his orange tabby
kitten, Charlie, locked out and meowing
on the doorstep. . . .

Honey
The abandoned puppy

When Eva finds Honey, a beautiful golden
retriever puppy, dumped on the doorstep of
Animal Magic, she's desperate to find the
lovable dog a new home. But Karl has other
ideas. He wants to follow the clue to find
Honey's real owner. . . .